FROM THE AUTHOR OF *BROWN BOY*

PILLAR OF THE KING

P.S. NISSIM

INDIA · SINGAPORE · MALAYSIA

"This one is for Dinks and Daddu.
Without you this book wouldn't have been."

It was only nine AM and already the heat was raising shimmering mirages on the highway ahead. Viren silently cursed the stuttering AC of his car as he steered northwards. Arpita, his wife, was more vocal. "We're all going to be tandoori chickens by the time we reach Hampi," she said.

"Didn't expect it to be so hot." He said.

Arpita straightened her five-foot frame in the seat. "Yeah, right," she said. "We were supposed to leave Bangalore by 5 AM sharp, but you're still eating breakfast at 5:30. These folks were waiting for us on time, so don't blame them." Viren pulled a sour face but didn't respond. Arpita hadn't finished taking her own medicine, either, but saying that out loud would have set her off. He focused on the road.

In the back seat, Puneeth startled awake with a jerk and rubbed his eyes. "Whazzza... how far did we get?" Ramya, his wife, gave him a glare. "You've been asleep for an hour... it's going to take a lot longer."

Puneeth looked around, yawning. "Who cares if it takes longer," he finally said, and settled back down. His belly, pushed out further by the motion, strained at the buttons of his florid shirt. "I was having such a strange dream…" He picked up a half-litre bottle of Thums Up that he'd tucked into the rear car door in the morning, and took a small swig.

Viren could see his tobacco-stained teeth in the rear-view mirror and suppressed a shudder. That was definitely not just cola in that bottle. Silently he cursed his fate. It was supposed to have been Ajay, Arpita's brother, on this trip with them. But Ajay had to drop out at the last minute, and the hotel had refused to refund the extra room.

He'd sent out the invitation on the society WhatsApp group, hoping someone would be available to join and pay his share. Most of the folks were decent, normal folks (like him and Arpita). Almost anyone would do.

But it had been the creepy drunk and his mismatched wife, of all people, who answered. No one else. Not one other person, who he could pull to the head of the queue. He cast another baleful glance at the cola bottle in the rear door slot. Even now this Puneeth was raving about that stupid dream of his…

"There was this girl, a teenager really, but very cute, and she was surrounded by snakes… holding them off with just a wave of her hand… looked like Sridevi in Nagina, she was ekdum…" Puneeth said. Impulsively his hands moved to shape a girl's body, until he noticed his wife's expression. "I mean, she was pretty…"

Ramya pointedly glared at him until he completely stopped talking and began looking out of the window at the desolate scenery outside. Then she went back to browsing her phone. The map said they were still a long way from Hampi, they'd probably get there way past sunset. These guys, Viren and Arpita, were probably going to just do the touristy thing and cover the main points. She'd send Puneeth off with them, while she got her own work done. A separate taxi to take her around, to get the sculpture photos her book project needed...

In the front row, Arpita was again asking how far they'd gotten. Viren was saying "– crossed Tumkur a while back, that was seventy km, and we'll stop to have lunch somewhere before Chitradurga - maybe when we're about halfway? A hundred and fifty odd?"

"Oh, can we stop at Chitradurga? It'd be good to take some pics of the fort," Ramya spoke up.

"You go up if you want," Arpita said resentfully. "I'm not walking around a stone fort in this heat. It'll set off the loose motions again."

Ramya noticed Viren's slight wince through the rear mirror. Hampi was probably going to be hotter than anywhere else, and the heat wouldn't be the worst thing about this trip from him...

They all fell silent. Arpita listlessly clicked through folder names in the MP3 drive, trying to find an album that she'd enjoy listening to. Ramya continued to scan her phone, Puneeth trying to doze off again.

Outside, the shrivelled trees flashed by. The four of them had all begun by watching the open scrublands in the morning, but the unremitting thirst of the land had sapped their interest. Occasionally a small village would appear, with its cluster of huts, an unadorned temple, and the mandatory speed bumps before and after it. Scrawny kids, their hair brown with dust, sat under trees watching a grazing goat or two. The sun beat down on everything, bleaching, killing, subduing it.

Viren looked again at the phone GPS. 4 hours to Chitradurga, it said. Ahead, the road sloped upward towards a hillock, dipping sharply and hiding beyond it. Right at the peak of the slope, next to the road, two small pillars stood out starkly against the blue sky.

Behind him, Puneeth called out, "Look, those are those fancy stones... Ramya, weren't you looking for them earlier?"

Ramya stirred a bit, looking ahead to see where Puneeth was pointing. "See, see – those ones... right?" Puneeth said, trying to draw her in. She nodded tentatively.

"I knew it! Hey, can we stop there? I need to take a leak, too." he said.

"Yeah, we'll wait in the car." Viren said as he maneuvered the car to the opposite side, parking it next to the pillars.

Puneeth rushed straight to the bushes nearby. Ramya began fiddling with her camera bag, taking out the camera, attaching the lenses, adjusting the strap... finally stepping out to walk, in no hurry, towards the pillars.

Viren watched Ramya go. She certainly had a nice figure... wonder how she'd married a bastard like Puneeth.

"High-and-mighty bitch," Arpita muttered. "Go on, take all the time you want, while we cook in here." She wiped a trickle of sweat off her brow. The car was sweltering already.

"Come on out, Arpu," Viren said, getting out of the car. She followed him after a moment.

Up close, the pillars seemed larger and more unkempt. Carved from black stone and about as high as a man, they were octagonal, with small carvings on the base. Ramya was photographing them close up, capturing the details, trying to get the writing. Viren looked closer. The script was some old language he couldn't read. Definitely not Kannada. Interspersed in between the words were drawings of snakes and scorpions. The bottom line of text was half-obscured by soil, and Ramya was wiping it away so she could get a good shot.

"Viren!" Arpita said suddenly, leaning back against the car. Her face was suddenly flushed.

Viren went back to her. "You feeling all right? Your face..."

Beads of sweat had broken out over her forehead. "Just feel very hot and uncomfortable," Arpita said.

"Stay in the car, then. Must be the sun."

"No, it's not the sun, it's –" Arpita cast a glance at the pillars and involuntarily shivered. "I don't like it here, Viren. Let's go?"

"Yes, let's go." The others were coming back, too. Viren turned on the ignition as soon as they were all in. Arpita was still shivering. Her face was white.

A horn blasted in the distance. A truck was speeding on the road behind them, rapidly catching up. Behind it, the dust rose in a cloud. Viren put the car in gear and moved it along the edge of the road, leaving space to let the truck overtake them.

The truck approached closer, and then blasted its horn in a series of deafening shrieks. The passengers in the car, startled, looked back. It was coming closer, threatening to run them off the road.

"What's it doing?" Arpita asked, her voice high pitched.

"Bloody fool, the road's too narrow for it to overtake…," Viren said, speeding up the car, looking for space to let the truck pass.

The truck let off its horn again.

"Whoa, slow down, Viren! We can't see–" Puneeth began.

Without warning, the road curved away to their right. The car, going too fast to control, skidded off the metalled surface, driving two wheels off the road. There was a loud *thunk* from the engine as the car ploughed through dust and slowed down.

The truck driver, apparently better in control of his vehicle, managed to take the sharp turn and overtake them.

"Bastard!" yelled Viren, at the retreating back of the truck. The car was now moving slower than ever, raising clouds of dust all around them and into the car cabin.

"What was that sound from the car?" Arpita said, coughing.

"Undercarriage hit the road's edge.... bastard!"

The car kept slowing down now - and a few seconds later, it stopped completely. "Shit!" Viren said. He gunned the starter, and the car started again, but it now moved feebly. A flapping sound came from somewhere in the engine, before it stalled for good. "Shit!" He said again, and got out.

Puneeth followed him after a moment. They opened the hood with some difficulty and stood there, looking in as smoke floated out of various parts of the engine. "Any ideas?" Puneeth asked. Viren just shrugged.

"Call the service people, Viren!" Arpita yelled from out her window. "Yes, yes!" He yelled back, phone in hand, already dialling.

He spoke briefly for a few minutes, describing what had happened, and where they were. The others listened to what they could. Yes, they were in between Tumkur and Chitradurga, somewhere. No, the car would not start now. Yes, Viren was willing to pay the extra fee for a highway rescue and repair. What did they mean, it would take 3-4 hours for them to get there? They'd die out here in this heat!

Viren looked around him as he spoke. Yes, he could see some sort of settlement about a kilometre ahead. Hang on - the map showed - yes, the place was a village called Thakshaka-stambha (what a weird name). Fine - FINE - they'd wait till the service vehicle arrived. He cut the phone connection, and wiped the sweat off his face.

They were all looking at him. He shrugged.

"They're gonna take more than four hours to get here." Puneeth said. "I vote we push the car to shelter nearby." He pointed to the village. "Only place available - Thak-shaka-whatever-it-is." From this distance it looked more - mechanical? - than a normal village, with cranes and a couple of brick kiln chimneys visible.

Arpita opened her mouth, but Ramya forestalled her with a quick "sure!", and began walking to the back of the car. Viren nodded, and followed her. Arpita, grudgingly, got out to walk alongside, while Puneeth took the wheel along with pushing the car, but not before taking a swig from his bottle.

It took them nearly half an hour. Arpita had stopped twice to drink water, and Puneeth had slipped and nearly fallen once. But now they were closer to the settlement, and Viren realized his first impression had been right: this was more of a construction site now. Something nagged at the back of his mind, however - some sensory impression that he hadn't quite processed yet.

There were at least half a dozen dump trucks moving around the place. A few of the houses looked like the typical village house, but they were overshadowed by a twin row of drab square huts set along one side - worker's quarters. Beyond those was a jumble of shanties made of tarpaulin, aluminium roofing, cardboard - the last refuge of construction workers at a site. On the far side of the village, they could see the jaws of two diggers suspended in the air. The bustle on the streets was all yellow-hardhatted workers as far as he could see. Several of them had stopped, staring at the newcomers curiously.

Viren looked around. Unpaved, dusty roads, and a single row of defunct solar-power streetlights. No chance of a hotel or restaurant. Up ahead there was a small temple, rather shabbily maintained, with what looked like a choultry behind it. The most interesting thing about the temple was the large pillar in the courtyard - black stone, looking more intricately carved than usual, oiled and well maintained in contrast to everything else around it. It reminded him of the marker stones they'd stopped to see on the highway.

"Yes, can I help you?" a voice said. He turned around to find a swarthy man glaring at him. The newcomer was middle-aged, dressed marginally better than the others, in a grey safari suit, but had the same kind of worker's helmet as the others.

"Er, yes - is this - " Viren looked down at his phone, " Takshaka...stambha? Our car broke down and the service centre guys told us to wait here. And my wife's not feeling well…" he gestured at Arpita, who was indeed looking pale.

"This is the place, but we're also a construction site for the dam." The man gestured vaguely towards the far side of the village. "There's no place to stay here." He continued in muttered Kannada, leaving Viren nonplussed.

Puneeth stepped into the conversation. "Hello, saar. I'm Puneeth. We don't really need to stay, just want to sit down in the shade somewhere, to wait a few hours."

The man turned to him. "Reporter aa?"

"Ille, saar! Just travelers. We were driving to Hampi and our car broke down. And she is not feeling well…" he gestured at Arpita.

The conversation continued in Kannada. From Puneeth's impassioned arguments, Viren gathered it was going well for them.

The man seemed to relent eventually. "Okay. Myself Reddy," he turned and addressed them all. "I'm the overseer for the project. Wait in your car if you want, or in the temple. Don't go around taking photos and irritating people here."

They didn't waste a minute after that. Pushing the car up to the temple, they washed their faces in the lukewarm water from the tap and settled down to wait in the shade of the lone tree in the stone-paved courtyard. Jasmine bushes around the periphery cast a light fragrance above the ever-present dust in the air.

"This would have been a nice village before the construction started," Puneeth said. "Nice of them to plant all these flower bushes there."

Ramya dug up a couple of packs of snacks from their luggage. "What we wouldn't give for a darshini here!" Puneeth said as they picked at the stuff.

As if triggered by the comment, a villager passed by them, bearing a plate with steaming idlis and chutney. This was the first person they'd seen without a hard hat, but otherwise he was dressed in dusty shirt-and-pants like all the others. Taking no notice of them, he went by, over to the choultry - two rooms constructed to the side of the temple, unimaginatively square and bland. Compared to the other structures, this seemed like a newer construction, with bright yellow paint on the exterior and modern-looking doors. The man rapped on one of the doors and waited.

"Is that where that Reddy guy lives? Guess he'd be the one to get royal treatment around here," Arpita said.

But it was someone else opening the door: a young girl, barely out of her teens, wearing, incongruously, a NASA T-shirt and blue jeans. Although her features were attractive, the bored, vacuous look on her face killed any attraction. She'd had her hair styled in a short fashion, made up her face with lipstick and some sort of rouge.

The man held out the plate of idlis. She gave it an uninterested glance, then finally took it and slammed the door shut in the man's face.

"Woah, that's one stuck up kid." Arpita breathed. Ramya turned to reply, then noticed Puneeth was staring at the closed door, with a strange intensity.

"Hello, mister!" Ramya said, pulling at Puneeth's ear. "What're you staring at?"

Puneeth shook his head as if to clear it. "It's strange, you know. I could have sworn that girl… that girl's the one I saw in my dream in the car…"

Viren had, in the meantime, already gotten up and was walking after the man, conversing with him in broken Hindi and what little Kannada he knew.

The two of them went quite some way down the street and around a corner. But when he turned back, Viren's face was all smiles. From a distance he gave two thumbs up, and gestured to them to come to him.

"He's agreed to feed us," he said. "Quoted a hundred rupees per person. He should see the prices in Bangalore sometime, heh."

They went down the street, rounded the corner, and stopped in surprise.

The village itself was built on a gentle hillock, and they were now across the peak and going down the other side. And now, finally, it was clear what was going on here.

The village sat on the edge of a sharp slope. Below them was a giant lake brimming with muddy water. Far across the valley, a sharp edge to the water showed where the dam was being worked on. A makeshift road zigzagged down the slope and along the water's edge up to the dam site.

They found the villager who'd offered them a meal. His wife had gotten a basic but filling meal ready: rice, sambar, a curry, and buttermilk. They sat down crosslegged on the floor to eat off banana leaves, traditional style.

Viren said after a few bites, "this is really excellent food. Thank you!"

The wife nodded solemnly and went back to the kitchen. The man came back out with a bowl of steaming rice to top up their plates.

"No, really, you should run a hotel here, people would come from far to eat!" He continued.

The man shrugged. "We're happy with this - the workers pay us well, and we'll move on to the next site when this construction is done."

Viren straightened. "What do you mean? Don't you live here?"

"For now, I do. The construction's been going on for two years now, and it may take another year. Once this is done, I'll move on to the next site with the crew. Cooking is my job."

"Oh," Viren said. "Somehow I thought you were a native of this place."

"No, I'm from near Belgaum. Everyone here is from outside, come to work on the dam. The actual natives are gone already - took their compensation and left. "

"Compensation?"

"Haven't you heard of this project? They're raising the height of the dam, so this whole village is going to get submerged. There was even a court case by the environment guys to stop it…all the newspapers wrote about it."

Viren was reminded of the strange question the contractor, Reddy, had asked Puneeth about being from the press.

"But apparently increasing storage capacity is important enough…Progress, Vikas and all that," the man continued. "So the government paid a hefty sum to the villagers. Made them leave. Then tried to get all cheaper workers from nearby villages.

"It didn't work, of course. Because of the legend."

"Legend?" Ramya had perked up. This was her thing.

"Yeah, you noticed the name of the village? Thakshakhastambha. You know who Thakshakha was, right?"

"King of the snakes? The Mahabharatha story with King Parkishit and all that?"

"Yes. I don't know if there's any connection, but this village has always belonged to the Havadigas, and others don't want to come here…"

He paused, shook his head. "That's why I'm here, because many of the workers came from other villages and didn't bring their families. And they took more money than the locals asked for. So the construction could happen. But it's not right. They shouldn't have destroyed this place."

"What are Havadigas —" Viren asked. But the man ignored him and continued, half to himself.

"The workers don't stay long, either. Even though contractor saab agreed to let that girl stay here to keep them happy."

That last sentence didn't make sense. Viren and Arpita both opened their mouths to speak, but Puneeth beat them to it. "What girl, that one you were giving idlis to?"

"Yes - that's Gowramma. She's the last one of the Havadigas left here, the workers insisted on someone staying back. She didn't want to stay, but they're pooling together to pay her some money, apparently."

"What is she doing here?"

The man considered for a moment, then shook his head. "Contractor saar doesn't like people to discuss it further, so I -"

But Viren's phone rang just then. "The car service guys!" he said. "Hello? Have you reached the pickup address?"

But the response from the other end did not sound encouraging, because his face fell. "What do you mean? That's too long! But where will we — Okay, can you at least try to make it earlier?.....So what am I supposed to say to that?"

He cut the line and looked around at them. "What?" Arpita said.

"They don't have any repair vehicles free right now, so they'll come tomorrow morning."

"WHAAAT!" She said, "Why didn't you tell them we're stuck in this no-name place and that your wife is sick?"

"What do I say, if they don't have any way of getting here, anyway?"

"But –"

"We'll just have to find a place to stay for the night, and hope they come tomorrow morning." Viren looked resolutely down at his plate and resumed eating.

Puneeth belched loudly and gestured to the cook. "Anna, we have a problem." he said. "We need a place to stay. Can you put us up here? We'll pay."

The man shook his head. "Some of the workers come and sleep here. No space left."

"You know anyplace else we could go to?"

"Talk to Reddy saar. He'll think of something."

"Maybe just the choultry? It's meant for travellers, no?"

"Gowramma is there - ask Reddy saar to arrange something else."

Puneeth opened his mouth to speak, but then shut it again. Arpita was looking mutinuous, but she didn't have anything to say, either. They finished the meal in silence.

After the meal, they asked the way to Reddy's cabin. They were led to a painted-over shipping container, with desk and chair inside, windows cut out on two sides, just a few metres from where the road dipped towards the lake. They found Reddy standing outside the cabin, smoking a cigarette and talking loudly to a couple of workers, gesticulating with his hands.

He saw them coming and paused, glaring at them as they approached. Puneeth said under his breath, "let me handle this."

"Reddy saar, we have a problem. Our car's workshop will send a person only tomorrow morning, so we need to find a place to stay for the night. Do you know anywhere we can sleep?"

"So, now I should find a hotel room, aa?"

"Nothing fancy - just beds for the night, we're fine with anything with a solid roof."

The man was looking at Arpita and Ramya up and down, his face growing red. "And you've got ladies with you so you won't stay with the workers, right?"

"Look, we're sorry about this, too - we didn't want to stay here, but there are four of us so we can't sleep in the car, and we don't have any bedding, otherwise we'd just have slept in the temple. We'll pay rent, if that —"

"Shut it! Already, the construction is behind schedule, the workers are all riled up and scared, and I've got my hands full keeping them together! Do what you want - go sleep in the temple or wherever. Don't bug me!"

Puneeth looked ready to argue, but Ramya grabbed his arm and pulled him away. Behind them Reddy called out again, "Listen, go to the choultry and ask that hi-fi madam - she'll be your best chance. I don't have any way to help you."

"Which way is the choultry?" Arpita asked.

"It was next to the temple. Look, over there, that black pillar." Ramya pointed. "Once we've figured out where to stay, I want to go look at it. Seemed like it had a lot of sculptures on it."

"First things first." Viren said. "Let's get you some rest, Arpu." They walked up the road again, towards the temple.

"There seem to be a lot of jasmine bushes on the streets, too," Ramya said. "You think they harvest them, sell them, or something?"

"Maybe," Arpita said. Her face was red again from the heat, and she was beginning to slow down. "But there are too many flowers on the bushes, and lots of dried ones on the road. Doubt they're picking the flowers."

They got to the choultry and knocked on the door. Up close, the building gave off a seedy air, as if no one cared for it any more, and no one would notice if it collapsed.

"Who is it?" The girl's voice came from inside.

"Er, we're visitors." Viren said. "Needed a little help."

There was a silence. Then, finally, the chain was unlatched from the inside and the door opened. The girl looked out suspiciously.

Up close she seemed younger than before, a teenager, the makeup some way to compensate for the innocence. A triangular bindi was tattooed on her forehead, and a snake motif tattoo encircled her bicep. She looked relieved, however, to see Ramya and Arpita, the suspicion giving way to curiosity.

"Yes, who are you?" She said in English.

"Hi, I'm Viren, this is my wife Arpita, and these are our friends Puneeth and Ramya. Our car broke down… we need a place to stay."

She seemed puzzled. "What do you want from me?"

"A couple of people here said the only place to stay is this choultry, and so we should ask you if you can spare some room for us."

She was looking closely at Arpita's red face. "Yeah, you can stay in the other room there," she said, pointing to a locked door further down the wall. "Wait here." Quickly slipping back in, she brought out a large rusty key on a ring.

They followed her to the door, then waited as she struggled to open it. Finally, Puneeth stepped up and forced it open. The room was musty, with old furniture, but there were big windows on two sides, and the ceiling was high enough to create some circulation. Another door was set into the far wall. There was only one double bed, but thankfully it had a mattress and sheets. "Puneeth and I will sleep on the carpet," Ramya said immediately.

"I have an extra mattress in my room if you need it." Gowramma said.

"Yes, that's great, thanks!" Puneeth said, giving Ramya a dirty look. He went off with the girl to fetch the mattress, and returned, huffing and puffing, hoisting it over his shoulder.

"Where does the back door go?" Arpita asked when they returned.

"There's an open area behind, with a toilet stall, and a well to fetch water. Pretty primitive, but your basic stuff gets done."

"You've lived someplace else before, right?" Arpita said. "You don't talk like a native."

"I used to be in Bangalore when I was a kid. Parents are still there. If I hadn't crashed out of college and made a mess of myself, I wouldn't be here today. Stupid villagers." Gowramma's mouth twisted as she spat out the words. "But just a few months more and I'll be done with this shit."

"Let's go get the luggage from the car," Puneeth said hastily. "You two stay here, girls."

As Viren opened the trunk, Puneeth asked him softly. "What's going on here? I thought she was some sort of whore."

Viren shrugged. "I don't know. She certainly seems well looked after here, and not exactly living against her will."

"Something strange, though. And somehow I still feel like my dream had her in it."

"Forget about it. And especially about this stupid dream thing. Place to sleep - done. Place to eat - done. Let's hope the service guys get here tomorrow and we're on our way in time. This place gives me the creeps."

"Yeah."

They hefted the luggage to their room. In the meantime, Ramya had struck up a conversation with the girl, and the three of them were sitting on the double bed, chatting. Arpita had managed to open the windows.

"There's a bit of a breeze from the lake, isn't there?" She said.

"Yes, it gets comfortable in the evenings and nights. You don't really need a fan," the girl replied.

"Hey, thanks for letting us stay here, Gowramma," Viren said.

The girl blushed a little. "That's all right. Considering that I'm the only native of this place left here, I suppose I have the responsibility for guests. Please call me Gowri - Gowramma feels like I'm a grandma."

"Why is that, though? I mean why did everyone else leave?"

She fell silent for a moment. "This whole village is going to be destroyed once the dam is ready, and the government paid for everyone to get a better plot of land further down the highway. Ten times the value of what this place is worth. Who'd be a fool to refuse that offer?"

"But then, why did you -" Viren began, but Arpita was glaring at him and shaking her head from behind Gowri. He stopped.

Gowri stood up. "Anyway, you guys rest a bit. We can have tea in the evening. Narayana will get it."

She went out the door. Viren turned back to Arpita.

"She was telling us she hates being here, but she needed the money," Arpita said.

"So…" Viren began.

"Yeah, you don't want to press her about how a girl is living alone at a construction site and earning money. Nor am I sure I want to spend much time with that sort of woman."

"What does that have to do with her being a native?"

"Look, you don't –"

"OK, stop. Who wants to come with me to look at the pillar?" Puneeth said. He stood up and began walking out the door. No one seemed too inclined to go out in the heat.

After a couple of minutes, he walked back in. "Ramya, need your help. There's a bunch of writing on the base of the pillar in your favourite language and you're the only one of us who can read it."

Ramya glared at him. "What language?"

"The old Halekanada you keep reading about in your course. This pillar's worth seeing."

"I'll come with you, too," Viren said. "Arpita, get some rest now."

Arpita raised a hand from her prone position on the bed. They latched the door gently as they left.

The pillar was, indeed, worth seeing. About two storeys high, made out of jet black stone, it was a roughly octagonal shape, with carvings all over it. From a distance, it had been hard to figure out what the carvings were, but now –

"They're all snakes!" Viren said. His face had gone pale. "I don't like snakes."

A large python carving encircled the bottom few feet of the pillar. Above it, snakes slithered up and down the sides, many with hoods spread. The quality of the carving did nothing to make Viren - and the others - feel any better. Below the python was a square platform, also black stone, about a foot high. Halekanada letters were carved into the sides.

"There, can you read that?" Puneeth pointed to the letters.

"I can try." Ramya knelt down and dusted off some of the writing with her hand. "It's really old-style Kannada, like the Vachana poems they had us learn in college. Starts with a year - in the Saka calendar, so that's.... What? Eighty years off, I guess... so that's about... wow, early 16th century. Five hundred years old!

"So this looks like a king or sponsor... Oh my goodness! It's an inscription about Krishna Deva Raya!"

"Anything about Tenali Raman?" Puneeth asked, and guffawed at his own joke.

"Shut up! It's… a land grant, I think. Says Krishna Deva Raya, the king, grants this village and all its creatures to the Ha-va-diga… that word again."

"That's us." A voice said from behind them. They turned. Gowri was standing there, arms folded. "It means snake charmers - that's our caste. It was supposed to be our village forever, where we ruled over everything. But now it'll be gone and there'll be no place to come back to." Her face screwed up a little, and she turned and walked away.

"Uh oh." Puneeth said.

Ramya was still reading the inscription. "But she's right, more or less. The village is willed to them for perpetuity, though the inscription says it was already tradition - because the Havadiga folks have been here with their creatures - why does it say creatures instead of snakes? - since always."

"Cool story, I guess," Puneeth said. "But the sculpture is more interesting."

"There's probably more nuance to the inscription, but I'm not good enough to catch it. Let's go visit the temple, too, while we're at it."

Viren looked around as they entered the shade of the temple. "You know, this place doesn't seem that old. Downright new, in fact."

The temple had looked solid from afar, but once inside, the shoddy quality of the construction showed.

Brickwork was still exposed at multiple places, and the garbhagriha walls were covered in rough cement. Nor was the idol - Balaji - anything more than a plaster-of-paris moulding.

They sat on the raised platform of the temple, legs dangling off the end. From here, they were facing a boundary wall, about ten feet high, painted in vertical white and brown stripes, the common pattern in many temples they'd passed on their way.

Puneeth looked around after a moment. Then, "that boundary wall looks taller than the walls on the other sides. Look!" They turned around, and indeed, the other walls looked dilapidated, and only about six feet high, compared to this one that they were facing. He jumped off into the courtyard, examining the wall as he went.

"There seems to be a double wall on this side, too - about six feet between this wall and the outer one. Must be a moat or some sort of fort defense."

But the walls were too high to look over, and so they hung around a few more minutes, getting bored, and then decided to walk back to the room.

The afternoon went by slowly. They sat around a couple more hours in the room, sweltering in the heat. Arpita had finally managed to doze off on the dusty bedcover, and Viren tried to do the same.

He knew he was asleep, because this felt like a dream. Viren was walking down the path outside their room, approaching the choultry. He was at their door, opening it, when there was a cry from further on. He turned quickly, to realize the cry had come from Gowri's room. With dream logic, he was instantly standing at her door, only to see her in the far corner of the room, terror on her face. The floor of her room was crawling with snakes, writhing and forming a moving carpet, inexorably congregating around Gowri, as she tried to get away. She noticed Viren standing at the door, and the look of mute appeal in her eyes was hypnotic. He looked down, and saw the snakes had noticed him too, were moving away, clearing a path between him and Gowri, inviting him to rescue her…

He jerked awake, sweating. He'd been afraid of reptiles all his life, to the extent of hating the tiny geckos in the gardens. And now, this weird dream, out of nowhere.

Beside him, Arpita was still asleep. He sat up feeling dazed, casting a wary glance around him. On the bed, Puneeth sat up suddenly, looking all around him with a startled look. Noticing Viren looking at him, he said quietly, "dream. Weird nightmare, nothing to worry about."

"Was it about Gowri again?"

Puneeth looked startled. After a moment, he said, "as a matter of fact, it was. Something like the dream I'd had earlier in the car. Gowri was there in the temple, and the ground around the temple was filled with -"

"Snakes?"

"Huh? How did you know?" Puneeth's face had gone ashen.

Viren slowly shook his head. "I had a dream like that, too. Snakes attacking the girl, she was looking to me for help, to rescue her… No idea where that came from."

"I don't get it."

Behind Puneeth, Ramya was waking up. "Too hot to sleep," she mumbled, rubbing her eyes.

"Let's walk around a bit, maybe go down to the water," Puneeth said. "Take our mind off things."

The three of them went out to wash their faces and freshen up by the well, and by the time they came back, Arpita had woken up. She decided to come along for the walk.

The sun was warm in their faces, without the fiery intensity of the afternoon, and hung above the hills beyond the lake. A breeze had sprung up. They strolled down the path, looking for a good spot to watch the sunset. Where the rows of houses ended, the road sloped downwards, zigzagging down to the water. Two trucks were coming up the slope. They moved a little way off the road and found a patch of grass interspersed with black rock to settle down on.

"It's quieter here than I thought," Puneeth said. "In the afternoon I thought the place would be full of construction sounds all day."

Ramya nodded. "It's almost as if we're back to when this was a normal village, with the original villagers still here. And the history of the place makes it feel really nice, like there's a land grant from the Vijayanagara times, and all that."

"Kind of nice that the workers still feel some of that traditional respect for the place, though, wanting someone from the original village to hang around."

"I told you, I don't think she's here just because she was from the original village - and I don't want you hanging around her too much," Ramya said sharply.

Puneeth was about to reply, when a conch rang out behind them, followed by a clashing of cymbals and a bell ringing. "I think it's coming from the temple," Arpita said. "An evening aarti, or something."

Viren stood up. "Well, I suppose we could go see it. Not much nightlife here."

They followed the sound to - as expected - the temple. A procession was exiting from the temple and going around the boundary wall. At its head was - unexpectedly - Gowri, clad in a traditional-looking costume with a blouse and pavadam, and silver jewellery that reminded Arpita of gypsies. But the bored expression on Gowri's face, Arpita thought, hadn't changed from the daytime.

The girl held out a small silver plate in front of her, with a burning lamp on it. Behind her, a middle-aged man in a white angavastram - probably the priest of the temple, followed by about twenty people discordantly playing cymbals, drums, bells, and some other wind instrument that she couldn't identify. Arpita focused as they got closer. From the typical appearance - a pipe with a bulging globe in the center, and the typical sound, she realized they were playing a snakecharmers' been. The procession was rounded off by half a dozen people carrying flaming torches. Arpita thought several of the people looked familiar - workers from the construction during the day.

The procession rounded a corner, and Arpita and the others followed at a distance. But as they too turned, they found that the group was going down a narrow staircase set in between the double walls of the temple - which hadn't been visible from the inside. The flickering lights of the procession played on the stone of the walls, slowly fading away, along with the sound, as the procession disappeared beneath the surface.

Viren said, "I don't know that I want to go down there." Puneeth nodded solemnly. And indeed, whatever was going on down there had already ended. People were coming out by ones and twos, carrying their instruments mutely or still holding on to their torches.

Last of all came up the two people who had been at the head - the priest, and Gowri. The priest continued on his way, but Gowri saw the four of them and brightened. "Hello there!"

She came over to them. "Bet you're wondering what was going on here. This is supposed to be the reason these guys want me to be here. Wanna see? Come on down!"

Viren looked at Arpita, who shrugged. They all followed Gowri as she went back down the stone staircase. By now, the crowd of the procession had completely dispersed and none of the locals was around. Gowri turned on her mobile phone torch as she went down to show the way into the darkness below.

The four of them turned on their phone lights, too, as they entered the room. It smelled strongly of moist earth and something more organic, something decaying. The walls were the same stone that the outside temple boundary had been made of, plain unadorned black stone, with the exception of a panel of wood in the far wall. The floor was just earth - and something else. From where they stood, there were metallic glints all over the floor. Puneeth bent down to look, and saw there were little iron and steel bits sunk into the earth. He prodded one of them. It didn't move - for some reason, it was stuck fast in place.

Gowri was standing there, grinning, waiting for them to get used to the light. "Welcome to my temple! Where I commune with the Gods directly! Every day!"

They continued to look around, trying to understand. Puneeth was busy poking at the metal bit in the ground.

"You don't get it, right? Because the whole thing is so stupid!"

She took out something from the side of her pavadam and held it out. "You know what this is?"

They came closer to look. It was a steel rod, bent into the shape of a U. The two ends were sharpened to points, while the bridge was flattened to about a centimetre wide. On the bridge, another rod was fastened. The whole thing was maybe a hands-length in size. Turned upside down, it would look like a Y, or a catapult. Or a tuning fork from school, with sharp points.

"No, what is it?" Puneeth asked.

"It's supposed to be a snake-catcher's hook, a Chimta," Gowri said. "Or at least a symbolic one. The temple has hundreds of these, made on contract by an ironmonger in a nearby village. There are lots of these in the earth here - look!" She pointed unnecessarily at the ground. Puneeth realized that the metallic bits had been the bridges of the U's, with the prongs embedded deep into the earth and the base of the Y protruding out.

"It's been a tradition in the village for centuries. Someone from our caste, a Havadiga, must put a chimta into the soil every dusk without fail. They've made a little ceremony out of it, too."

"But, but, why? What's it for?" Ramya broke in. "I haven't heard of this ceremony anywhere else."

Gowri shrugged. "Neither have I, but the villagers here - and now even the construction workers who came after them - believe it wards off evil or something. They're willing to pay money to have it done. Fortunately I was available. A few months more of this, and I'll have them find someone else and use the money to start a boutique in Bangalore."

Arpita was staring at her, somehow unable to believe the story. "And... that's all you're here for? To put this stupid spike into the ground once a day?"

Gowri gave her a sharp look. "You think I'm a whore, huh? I've been seeing it in your eyes all day. Says something about what your mind is like.

"Well, listen - these people are too scared of the local gods to touch me, okay? They think I'm a sort of priestess here just because of my background, even if I've never handled even an earthworm in my life. I'm safer here than I'd be anywhere in the world. Except when holier-than-thou drama queens like you come around, judging me."

Arpita seemed to wilt with every sentence. "No, I didn't think that… I mean, what would anyone think…" Even in the flickering light of the phones, her cheeks were flaming red.

Puneeth spoke up. "Hey, Gowri, this is all very cool, though. Obviously, who are we to judge what goes on in the villages, right? If they're willing to pay for something, why not?"

Gowri was silent for a moment. Then evidently deciding to lump herself with them instead of with the villagers, she nodded, and said, "I don't want to diss the rituals, they've been going on for centuries… but I needed the money. Doesn't make me a bad person."

Ramya pitched in. "Of course not. Hey, listen, what are you doing now? If the whole thing is over, want to join us for a few drinks and snacks? I was thinking, I have a few movies on my laptop, we could watch something and chill out."

Even Arpita nodded enthusiastically. Gowri smiled after a moment. "I'd like that. It gets really boring in the evenings here."

They filed out of the narrow chamber and trooped to their room. Ramya began to turn on the laptop as the others cleared out the bed and pulled up a small table to act as the stand.

"So we have Jaani Dushman, Nagina, and Naagin… which one should we see?" Puneeth said, grinning. Gowri just looked confused, but Ramya gave him an exasperated glare. "Quit kidding, Puneeth - So I have the new Salman Khan movie for timepass, and the new Ayushmaan Khurana one, and then…" she reeled off a few movie names and let Gowri make the choice for them all.

They arranged themselves around the laptop, some on the bed and the rest on chairs, feet up on a table or a duffel bag. Gowri seemed completely mollified and enjoying herself now, joining in passing the mandatory silly comments and jokes that every Salman Khan movie requires.

Half an hour later, Viren got up to get a drink. The ice in the cooler had all melted by now, but the beer was still a little cooler than room temperature. "Anyone else wants one?" He asked as he opened his bottle.

Unexpectedly, Gowri's hand shot up. "Me, me!" She said gleefully. Then abashed, she said, "that is, if you guys are okay with sharing."

"No, why not - here," Viren said, as he passed on the bottle in his hand and opened another one."

"Hang on - Gowri, how old are you?" Arpita asked sharply.

Gowri giggled a little. In the dim yellow light, she seemed like a schoolgirl. "I finished college last year, Arpita - I just look younger. Don't worry about me…"

She took a swig. "It's been a long time. No one here will get me a drink, old-world bastards…

"You wouldn't have any Old Monk, would you?"

"Um, I do," Puneeth said. "Though I'm not sure how the people outside will take a full-blown drinking party here."

"No one needs to know! I at least am not going to tell," Gowri said, almost jumping up and down in glee. "Oh, how I've missed a good Old Monk and coke!"

Puneeth hesitated a moment more, scanning the faces of the others for any hints. No one seemed against the idea.

"Oh, let's have a round," Viren said. "It's been a long day."

He set up a bunch of paper glasses while Puneeth took out the bottle from his backpack. The Thums Up with it was room temperature but would do.

Gowri insisted on getting some kodubale and mixture from her room. "Let's have a proper party!"

They started the movie again, but Arpita broke out in giggles within a few minutes, when Salman dropkicked a goon through a window. It triggered something in all of them - a sense of relief, or at least of putting aside the day's stress, and they fell into conversation.

"So, what did you do in Bangalore, Gowri?" Ramya asked.

"I got a scholarship to Christ College, and then joined a call centre… but I didn't like it at all," Gowri said. "They kept making fun of me for being a villager, a bumpkin,… all sorts of stuff."

"But you don't seem any different from any other college kid, really."

Gowri said nothing, but her face brightened a little. She took a big sip of her paper cup.

The conversation moved on to other topics then, the way such conversations do… movies, music, comparisons of Dr. Rajkumar with Kishore Kumar, favourite places for chaat in Bangalore,…

The bottle was almost over, between the five of them, yet no one was willing to call it a day, least of all, Gowri, who seemed a totally different person from the morose girl they'd seen in the afternoon.

"… but after all, if you're a professional and want to do good work, you will wind up in Bangalore eventually!" Viren was saying. "I wanted to stay in Ahmedabad for the longest time, but Arpita wound up with a job here, and I must say it was a good decision for us both to come here. Ahmedabad is a dead city, man… nothing to do there at all!"

"Yes, I love Bangalore, too…" Gowri said. "I had the best years of my life there… if only…"

"But what stops you now? Who told you you can't drop all this and go back to the city?"

"I… promised my mother, and the priest… and they're paying me money…" But Gowri's voice, fuelled by the drink, no longer seemed happy about the situation.

"You shouldn't let other people dictate your life!" Arpita put in. "Even between Viren and I, I have as much right to make decisions! Ask Viren!"

"True, very true!" Viren said. "This isn't the old times, or a Saas-Bahu serial, for God's sake!"

Gowri was nodding her head slowly. "I hate it here! And I don't want to live my life as a cheap scam to get money from villagers! Whoops!"

She'd squashed the paper glass too hard in her hand as she spoke, and spilled some of the drink onto her jeans. "I'll be back," she said, as she hurried back to her room.

For a moment, the room was silent. Arpita quietly said, "I feel sorry for her."

Ramya said, "But let's not keep piling it on and making her feel bad, all right? She's still a kid, doesn't understand everything. Maybe her family needs the money."

"Yeah, true."

"Let's just watch the movie. Don't provoke her, now."

They waited till Gowri was back and then restarted the movie as if nothing had happened.

It was past midnight when it was over, and thankfully, the bottle of Old Monk was over as well. The conversation went around to the movie stunts again, and they spent a little time arguing over whether it had been a good choice. But Gowri claimed she'd found it fun in a stupid way. "I just enjoyed spending time with you guys! It doesn't happen often enough."

"We should get to sleep now," Arpita said.

"But I don't feel sleepy at all," Gowri said. A moment later, she let out a huge yawn. "Ok, maybe I do. You got me!" This last, drunkenly pointing finger pistols at Arpita. "I was wrong about you, Arpita…. You're a very wise woman… a very wise woman!" She swayed.

"Do you want me to help you back to your room?" Viren asked.

"No, no, I'll make it. Good night, everyone! And in case we don't meet in the morning, hopefully your car repair guy comes through in time!" She stumbled a little bit crossing the threshold, and noisily made her way to her room further down the building. They could hear her opening the door and then slamming it shut.

"Well… that was that." Viren said.

"Was a reasonably fun evening, even if we didn't get to Hampi," Ramya added.

"Right. And now, off to sleep." They bustled about for a bit, brushing teeth, putting down phones to charge, figuring out blankets, and finally, turning the lights off.

Outside, it was eerily quiet, with not even the sound of crickets. Far off in the distance, the occasional sound of trucks on the highway could be heard, the only background sound available.

Sometime in the night, Viren was startled awake by Arpita shaking him. "Hsst, Viren, wake up! Wake up!"

From the other side of the room, Ramya asked sleepily, "what happened?"

"There's something in the bathroom!"

Viren, by now awake, sat up. "What is it?"

"Something in the bathroom! I think... it's a snake!"

"WHAT!" He stood quickly. Behind him, Puneeth was turning on the room light. "Wait here, I'll check it out," he said. Ramya came up to Arpita and Viren, standing close by for reassurance.

Puneeth had picked up a shoe in one hand, slowly moving toward the bathroom door. With the reassurance of the others around her, Arpita was now shuddering. "There, it's okay," Viren was telling her, though he felt sick in the pit of his stomach.

Puneeth opened the door cautiously. "Where did you see it?" He called out. "In the corner, behind the bucket," Arpita said. "Big, black thing..."

They watched him as he stepped into the bathroom. There was a scraping sound as he moved the bucket around. Then, a moment later, he called out, "nothing in here!"

He came out himself and glared at them all. "You cowards let me go in there alone? What if it had been there, ready to strike?"

"I hate reptiles, you know that," Viren said. The other two, white faced, just shook their heads.

"Yeah, yeah. Anyway, there's a drainhole in that corner, and I see some fresh earth around it, so perhaps there was a snake and it came in through the drain. Anything here to block the drain with?"

They wound up putting on the teak side tables, sideways, to block off the drain with a full bucket of water on top to weigh it down. Puneeth did most of it, with Ramya grudgingly helping him carry the table into the bathroom. "No one takes a bath here tomorrow!" he announced after the table had been fitted in place.

"Not interested in baths, anyway," Viren muttered. He'd been in a state of near-panic ever since he'd woken up. "The sooner the repair guys get here and fix the car, the better."

Even after the light was switched off, Viren remained awake for a while, glancing nervously at the closed bathroom door every now and then. Outside, it was even quieter than before, the sound of distant trucks screeching and gunning their engines feeling louder in comparison.

Viren looked at Arpita. She'd fallen asleep in a few minutes, apparently reassured by the table-blocking exercise. But Viren knew the truth. He'd seen a nature documentary once, in which a snake had gotten out of a closed box through an unbelievably tiny hole. The table probably wouldn't stop anything that really wanted to get into the room.

A faint sound reached him, of people talking loudly, off in the distance. He checked his phone. It was past three. Too early for a construction shift to start? Then again, he hadn't heard any construction equipment start up. Maybe they were just waking up now.

The sounds increased in volume, a little more, the voices sounding harsher as they came closer. Viren got up and went to the window. A couple of lights bobbed off in a street, behind the first row of houses. As he watched, the lights broke up into two groups, one - smaller - group going off towards the scrub bushes on the edge of the villages. Another group was coming in his direction. The temple, maybe, he thought. The group passed by their compound and, indeed, went over to the temple, passing out of his range of sight.

A moment later, there was a loud banging sound. Viren remembered that the temple priest had had a small cabin just behind the temple. He heard the rattle of a chain, and a rectangle of light appeared and stretched out on the ground where he could see. Agitated voices began talking, in Kannada.

"What's going on?" Puneeth said quietly behind him, making him jump.

"I don't know. Something happened further down in the village, I think, and some people have come to talk to the priest."

Puneeth leaned forward a bit, trying to listen in.

"They're blaming the priest for something, some pooja he didn't do properly," he said, still listening.

"Something strange…. They're blaming him for a dog getting lost! It wouldn't have gotten lost if he'd done his job properly…

"Not lost - carried away is the phrase they're using."

"Carried away? By what?" Viren asked, voice tremulous.

Puneeth shook his head. "The priest is protesting… saying everything is all right…" But suddenly there was the sound of someone else running up to the group from down the street, shouting something in a panicky voice.

Puneeth frowned in confusion. "He's shouting, 'they're coming for us! They're coming for us in the night! What did you do wrong?' "

"What does he mean?"

In response, the priest's voice rose, too. The new arrival continued to talk loudly in between gasping breaths.

"This is bad," Puneeth said. "It looks like a child has disappeared, now."

"Children, here?"

"From a worker's family, I think."

A large portion of the group now broke away, brandishing torches and mobile phones. They followed the later arrival back towards the village.

"I think we should go help them…" Puneeth said.

"Help them do what? We don't know anything here!" Viren said, taking an involuntary step back.

"They're going out into the bushes to look for the kid. All it needs is a torch." Puneeth seemed to be taking a decision.

"Puneeth, do you really need to go?" Ramya asked from behind them. "I get that you want to help, but we don't know if they want your help…"

"Let me just see what's going on," Puneeth said, "and if there's nothing we can do, I'll be back. You guys get some rest."

Without waiting for an answer, he dug out a jacket from his bag, and a small torch, and opened the door. "Close this after I go," he told Viren. "Sleep if you can."

"Look, take care, dude," Viren said. Puneeth nodded as he went out.

Puneeth caught up to the group of people as they reached the end of the street. They knew of him already. "I heard a boy went missing, you need help with finding him?" He asked in Kannada.

A middle-aged man in the group, still incongruously wearing a construction hat, said, "Yes, come. But be careful, we still don't know what happened here."

"What do we know?" Puneeth said, falling into step along with the man. The group was about a dozen strong now, most with a mobile phone torch lighting up the way ahead. A few had lathis in their hands, too.

"The boy was carrying some food from his home to a relative's home down the street. Someone heard him cry out loudly, along with some animal sounds, when they looked out, the boy was gone, and there were some strange tracks by the side of the path."

"What kind of tracks?"

"I don't know, I only just heard all this. That's where we're going now."

The group had reached almost the end of the street, where a few others were waiting for them. Lights were on in all the houses, Puneeth saw as he walked, but not too many people were out.

One of the waiting men gestured towards the ground as they approached. Puneeth, along with the others, stopped to look.

The grass and bushes at one place next to the kaccha road had definitely been disturbed, with broken stalks and leaves scattered on the ground, but it wasn't clear what kind of animal it had been. But there was a large streak of mud on the road itself, as if something muddy had been dragged along for a bit. They looked at it for a minute.

Eventually someone said, "I don't see any pugmarks or hoofmarks."

"It won't be a tiger or leopard, we'd have heard it roaring at some point." The middle-aged man said.

"Let's follow the tracks into the jungle, maybe the boy is nearby. Whatever animal it is, will run from a crowd."

There were a few sceptical, frightened faces, but eventually the people drew strength from their numbers, and began following the trail into the forest. Puneeth stayed close to the middle-aged man, the de facto leader. To him, the trail wasn't that clear, but the villagers seemed to be able to follow it fairly easily. The jungle - really scrubland with thorny babool bushes and the occasional tree - was quiet. Was it supposed to be this quiet? Puneeth wondered. Perhaps because it was the deepest of night, there were no birds or small animals anywhere. The occasional broken branch and torn leaf continued to lead them deeper into the jungle.

Puneeth got scratched several times by babool thorns, before he followed the villagers' lead and pushed the branches cautiously out of the way. The group was moving slowly, Puneeth trying to make out the trail as the leader pointed out markers.

Something flashed in the grass, ahead of them. There was a collective gasp, as the men retreated. A moment later, Puneeth too recognized it - a large black snake, slithering swiftly through the undergrowth, crossing their path. It moved beyond the narrow reach of their lights, was audible for a second more, and then was gone.

A man whispered behind Puneeth, "How did that get here?" A murmur of agreement broke out around him.

"Why? This is the jungle, isn't it?" Puneeth was pressed to say.

"Not in our area, we're under protection…" the middle-aged man replied to him.

It seemed to Puneeth that the party grew suddenly ambivalent about going on. Their progress was now more hesitant, everyone looking around more nervously, as if they were in strange territory.

"It was just a snake, right?" He pressed.

No one responded. They continued to look around carefully, pointing their lights this way and that.

"I mean, you have them in jungles and villages…" he tried to think of something more to say. "Like, we had one in our room today morning, too -"

"What did you say?"

All at once he had their complete attention. They'd stopped looking around and were staring at him.

"What? Just a snake in the bathroom drain. Didn't do anything to us, it went back when we were close."

Their faces were white with fear. "It went back, huh? Soon they won't – go back." Someone said.

Without any further discussion they turned back towards the village, hurrying, not bothering to check whether Puneeth was keeping up with them.

"We should go talk to the poojary," the middle-aged man was saying as they went. The group continued down the lane, past their houses, and towards the temple. The priest was still standing outside, talking to a couple of people in a quiet voice. Noticing them coming back, and their grim faces, he assumed the worst.

"Did you find the boy? Is he - " he began.

"We saw a snake," the middle-aged man said. "Just a few minutes outside the village. And these people -" gesturing towards Puneeth, " had a snake in their room - in their room! Just a couple of hours ago!"

The priest went pale as well. "But that's not... possible. We did the ritual today, just like every day... you all saw it. Unless..." his gaze went towards the choultry just beyond the temple.

"What are you people talking about..." Puneeth said, but now the group, led by the priest, was moving towards the choultry. Puneeth braced to take some action if something weird happened, but the group continued beyond their room and stopped at Gowri's room. The lights were off there. The priest rapped sharply at her door.

There was no sound from inside. He repeated the knock after a minute, to no effect.

The middle-aged man turned to Puneeth and said, "Are you sure there was a snake in your room?"

"In my bathroom, yes, pretty sure. I saw the mud tracks." Puneeth said. "But really - what's going on? What does Gowri have to do with anything here? She was with us last night..."

For the second time that night, Puneeth's words had an electric effect on the group of men. Amidst the sudden silence, the priest turned to him, and asked, "So you were the last people to see her last night?"

"Um, I don't know? We watched a movie together and she went back to her room after that…"

Someone murmured under their breath, and Puneeth couldn't make out what they were saying.

The middle-aged man seemed to come to some conclusion. "Show me where the snake appeared in your bathroom."

Puneeth stared at him. "I don't know what that will solve. But yeah, sure, come along and I'll show you."

He led the way back to his door and knocked. Viren opened it, looking doubtfully at the men standing behind Puneeth.

"What's going on?" Viren asked in a low voice.

"Nothing, this guy just wants to see where the snake came from, in our bathroom last night. Are the others up?"

"Yeah, none of us has been able to sleep. And also… never mind, I'll tell you in a bit."

Puneeth stepped in, expecting a couple of the others to come in with him. To his surprise, no one came. He turned around, to find the middle-aged man further away, in heavy conversation in hushed tones, with two of the others. He called out, "Hello saar - you wanted to see where the snake was?"

In answer the man nodded vaguely, raising his hand in a coming-in-a-minute gesture, and continued to talk. The others were nodding at something he said. Then they turned and purposefully walked into the room.

Something was wrong, Puneeth sensed. They were looking around, evaluating the place, their gaze stopping on the empty glasses on the side table from the night. Behind him, Arpita and Ramya were awake, too, and had retreated to a far corner of the room.

"It was in the bathroom, near the drain… this way," he said, trying to lead them that way.

The middle-aged man stepped up purposefully to Puneeth and Viren, and put out a hand. "Your phones." He said in halting English.

"What? Why do you want…"

"Give me the phones! You people seem to have caused enough trouble already here. Give!" the man continued in Kannada. He raised the staff in his hand in warning.

Arpita screamed. The two other villagers had stepped closer to them, and had said something similar.

"Look, sir, we don't want trouble - if you don't want us, we will leave now," Puneeth said, hands help up to placate them.

"Too late for that. Where is Gowramma? Where have you sent her?"

"Gowri? We haven't done anything to her! She was in her room only, last we saw…" Puneeth said. Sweat had appeared on his forehead.

"Liar! She isn't supposed to leave the village boundary, and she knows it! She knows of the contract!"

"But - "

"Stop this nonsense! With your phones, you will cause more trouble! Give your phones!"

Arpita screamed again from behind them. Viren shouted out, "What are you doing! She's not well!"

"What happened?" Puneeth turned to him.

"She's developed a fever during the night…"

Puneeth nodded, and translated for the villagers. It didn't seem to have any effect.

"All right - hold on…" Puneeth gingerly took out his phone and held it out. "Take it - take it. Viren, girls, give them your phones."

"But… what's going on, Puneeth? What happened outside?" Ramya asked him.

"I don't know… we'll figure it out later…"

Viren took out his phone, and his wallet, and held it out. "Here, take it, take our money, just let us go…"

The man looked angrily at Viren for a second. Then he brandished his lathi, shouting, "You think we're robbers! You idiot!" Viren cowered at the threat, not understanding.

The two girls had, in the meantime, taken out their phones and handed them over. The leader gathered the phones into a plastic bag and held it tightly. "Stay in here while we figure out what to do!" He waggled the lathi again at Viren, and then he and the others left the room.

"Wait! Tell us what you're doing! We can help you find Gowri, if that's what you want!" Puneeth shouted, coming up behind them - only to have the door slammed and locked in his face.

"Hey! HEY!" Puneeth went to the window, shouting. The group of men had moved beyond their room, but had stopped apparently just beyond their sight, behind the temple. An argument was going on there again. Puneeth tried to listen in, but could make out nothing much more than he already knew.

Finally he came back to the others. Arpita was lying down on the bed, surrounded by Ramya and Viren. She looked pale and weak.

"She's got a fever now, I think it's increased in the last hour or so." Ramya said.

"Why are they locking us up? What's going on?" Viren asked.

Puneeth paused for a moment, trying to put it all together. "I think there's some superstitious thing here about snakes not allowed in the area, and they think that us coming here has broken some taboo."

"And where does Gowri fit into it? I heard them mention her," Ramya asked.

"She was the one that did the pooja every day, but... For that matter - does anyone know where she is?"

They looked at each other. After a moment, Arpita spoke. "I think she's left town."

"Huh? What?" Viren looked down at her, surprised.

"We chatted a bit last night, just before the movie ended. She told me she wanted my number, and I gave it to her. She said she might contact me when we got back to Bangalore."

There was silence. "She said, she'd contact us when *we got back*, not when she got there," Arpita repeated. "I didn't realize it then."

"So you think she left right after she went back to her room?"

"Could be. All your prompting about living her life where she liked…" Arpita's face was even paler now. She shot a venomous glance at Puneeth.

"Plus the Old Monk," Viren put in.

"Guys - we're all stuck here together, no point blaming each other now!" Ramya said, as Puneeth glared back at the other two.

"We don't even know what we've triggered off here!" Viren shouted.

"I - wait. I can put this together," Puneeth said, backing away a little. "Gowri leaves the town last night. Right after, they see a couple of snakes in the neighbourhood, and one snake comes into our room, and everyone panics. That one guy told me a contract had been broken, when Gowri left the village… maybe the pooja was supposed to keep snakes out. Havadigas, remember." He shrugged and sat heavily. "Maybe it was just bad luck, a couple of snakes being seen just when we happened to be around."

"And the kid who got carried away in the night?" Viren asked. "It's not all coincidence."

"Who knows?" Puneeth replied. "This is a village, next to a jungle. Animals attack people all the time. No one could figure out what animal took away the kid, but there were definitely tracks of *something* - it wasn't like a ghost or monster."

The dawn light was streaming across the room by now. Outside, there were sounds of activity and talk in the distance. Puneeth got up and went to the window again, hoping someone would come by. But he could only see people moving back and forth in the village streets, no one paying attention to the choultry. He tried stretching out his hand to see if he could reach the door latch, but it was too far away.

"There's one way to get out for us," Ramya said suddenly.

Everyone turned to her.

"The car mechanic should be coming to the village soon - we'd called them, right?"

Viren brightened at the thought. "Yes, they'd said they'd be here in the morning." He looked at his watch. "Around 11 or 12, he'd said."

"Except we don't have the phone to receive their call, if they want to contact us in the meantime." Puneeth said. "But yes, the car is right here, around the corner from the temple. If they fix the car, we should just get out of here."

"But I still don't get what the point of locking us in here is," Ramya continued. "I mean, if we're troublemakers and causing hassles here, making their pet pooja girls leave and all, they should want to get us out of here, right?"

Puneeth nodded. "If only someone would come here and we could talk to him. If they just want Gowri to come back here for their daily ritual, I could try and talk her into it… just pay her more money."

"No… it's… too… late…" Arpita suddenly spoke up from the bed. She'd been quiet so far, semi-conscious in her fever. Viren put a hand to her forehead and recoiled. "Her fever's really gone up!" He said.

Arpita shook his hand off. "No, listen… I heard them talking when I was… asleep. The village is theirs again… now that the snake catchers are… gone."

"Arpita, what are you talking about?" Viren said. He held her hand in between his, trying to reassure her of his presence.

But she wasn't looking at them. Her eyes were focused far off on the horizon, as if still seeing some nightmare. Her forehead was beaded with sweat now. "Them… I saw them, there were hundreds, lakhs of them… all waiting for hundreds of years…"

"Arpita! Look at me!" Viren shouted. "Arpita!"

Her eyes focused back on Viren. "There were so many snakes, Viren… in their kingdom, below the earth, all happy to be free…" she shuddered. "Was it just a dream?"

"You have a fever, Arpu," Viren said, gently massaging her forehead again. "It was just a dream. I think you should take a Crocin or something…" he looked up at Ramya and Puneeth. Ramya hastened to her bag, where she had a small stock of tablets for the trip. She brought it back to the bed, while Viren helped Arpita sit up, and swallow the tablet with a few sips of water.

"We really have to get out of here," Viren said quietly. "I don't know how. Maybe we can get to the highway, and hitch a ride on the trucks going - "

Outside, there was a sudden clamouring again, people shouting in panic. Puneeth went again to the window, to see a mass of people rushing away from the village streets, crossing close to the temple and the choultry as they went.

"Hey! Hey!"

No one stopped for them. It looked like they were running away from something. Puneeth heard someone shouting, "I saw it, I tell you!" as they went by, but couldn't get anyone to stop and explain.

"At this rate, the village will be empty soon," Ramya said. She had found a small towel and was setting up a cold compress for Arpita.

Puneeth tried again to reach the latch of the door from the window, and as before couldn't reach anywhere close.

Viren stood up and began looking around, too. The window was barred with thick iron bars and a sturdy frame. Besides the one door and the window, there didn't seem to be any way out. He scanned the room.

The bathroom - he thought of the smaller window above the toilet there, and unlatched the bathroom door to check it out. He'd only taken a step inside, when he became aware that he wasn't alone in the room.

A large black snake - a cobra? - was coiled on the floor, not far from the drain.

Viren felt his blood go cold. The snake looked almost two metres long, black and shiny, and it was moving slowly towards the entrance.

He shut the door as fast as he could, slamming it in his haste. "It's in there!" He shouted, voice quivering as he backed away from the door and pushing himself into the far corner of the room.

The others turned uneasily to look at the door. Because Viren hadn't bolted it - and the slammed door was now creaking open under its own weight. Lazily, in no hurry, it went on opening. Something was moving inside the bathroom, too.

There was now something, a deeper shadow on the floor next to the bathroom, Puneeth saw.

No, it wasn't a shadow. Shadows didn't slither along the ground, taking up more space as more of them appeared, at least a half dozen of them, the snakes wisping out of the bathroom like tendrils of black steam out of a pot...

He cast a quick glance at the others. Viren was pale, his face beaded with sweat, while Ramya was holding her place by Arpita's bedside, just barely. Arpita seemed ready to faint, half sitting on the bed, pushing herself to the far end of the bed, her face ashen, otherworldly terror in her eyes.

For a moment, the snakes continued to come out from the bathroom. The one right in front, a larger, black specimen, seemed to be the leader - did snakes move in packs like this? Puneeth thought. Behind the black one, a half-dozen others, with various stripes and patterns, followed. He thought he recognized a Russell's Viper, and one, was it a cobra or a rat snake? The websites told you to check for the marking below the eye to know, he thought crazily, as if anyone was going to go close and look at its eyes…

Abruptly the black snake stopped. It raised its head – was that the hood - in the air about six inches and looked around the room. Puneeth tried to figure out something nearby that he could use as a weapon if they got too close. It would be useless, of course, the creatures were lightning-fast and there were too many of them… but the other snakes had stopped behind the leader.

The snake was looking - yes, indeed, it was looking directly at Arpita now. As if it recognized her and had been searching for her. Arpita's face grey and wet from sweat, as she stared back at the snake for a long moment. Then, overcome, she fell back in a faint. Ramya's hands moved frantically, massaging Arpita's single hand in hers, but her eyes stayed focused on the group of snakes.

Then, as if they were listening to a message from somewhere, the snakes flattened onto the ground, turned around, and went back into the bathroom. In less than a second they were out of the room. A rustling sound came from the bathroom for a few seconds more, then all was silent.

"What… what just happened" Viren said shakily.

"I don't know," Puneeth said. Ramya was still sitting there, staring at the open door of the bathroom. Puneeth took a step towards it, and Ramya instinctively called out, "Don't!…"

"I'll be okay," Puneeth said, cautiously approaching the door. As he'd suspected, the bathroom was empty, no sign of the reptiles anywhere. A few marks remained on the floor, like the ones he'd seen earlier around the drain. He was suddenly reminded of something.

"Hey," he said, stepping back into the main room, "You remember earlier, they couldn't figure out what animal's tracks they were?"

Ramya looked at him, questioning.

"Because they were so blurred. But I'm looking at the tracks in the bathroom, and…"

Ramya's hand had shot up to her face in horror. "But… would there be snakes that big? To pull a child off the street…?"

"I don't know. But what's normal here? Snakes moving in packs? Arpita dreaming… visions? What was that, even?"

"Puneeth. We need to get out of here, quickly." Viren was saying. He was still standing against the wall, as far from the bathroom door as he could get, his eyes straying back to the door as he spoke.

"I know, but how? There's no opening here."

"What if we… kicked at the door or something?"

"Doubt it. It's one of those solid, old fashioned teak doors." Puneeth looked around the room again, not seeing any way out.

"But then what? Do we just stay here until we starve to death, or -" Viren's voice was rising in panic.

"Could we try the roof?" Ramya cut in.

"What do you mean?" Puneeth was asking her, but as he looked up, he could see her point. The roof of the building was sloping, made with clay roofing tiles, and supported by a wooden framework. There seemed to be a lot of dust and spiderwebs, but that would be easy to manage.

"Yeah, I see that…" he continued. "We need to find a way to get up onto something, like a bed or… chairs…"

"Arpita can't climb that! And I don't like heights…" Viren protested.

"Just needs to be one person, unlatching the door from outside. It has to be you, Viren. I can't pull myself up there," Puneeth said

"Don't drag me into your inane plans, you fucking freeloader! I could break my arm!"

Puneeth's nostrils flared. "Goobe, you're the one who's scared of snakes and wants to get out! You have a better idea?"

"Ask Ramya to do it if you –"

"Viren!" Arpita called out wearily from the bed. Her eyes were still closed.

Viren paused. His shoulders drooped. "Fine. Fine! You two had better hold the table properly."

The three of them dragged a desk and two tables over to the wall by the door. Puneeth was already out of breath. They aligned the smaller tables on top of the stack quickly.

"Here goes," Viren said, testing the topmost table for stability. "hold it tight while I get up," Viren said.

Viren gripped Puneeth's shoulder and clambered onto the first, then the second table. His head knocked against the wooden rafters as he gingerly stood up.

"So far, so good," he called out as he stabilized himself by holding onto the beams. The dislodged dust made him cough.

"Can you reach the tiles?"

"Yes, I think I can." Viren said, and stretched out a bit to touch the clay tile. "Yes."

"Pull out a tile and pass it to me, careful now!"

Viren put out both hands and tried to grab the clay tile. But it was damp and slimy on the underside, and he only managed to get it out of its place, before it slipped out of his hands, and went slithering down the roof. A moment later, they heard it crash to the ground.

Viren stopped for a moment, his heart thudding, listening for any commotion as a result of the falling tile. The light from the hole now fell across his face and the wooden beams, making it easier to see the other tiles.

"Doesn't look like anyone heard us," Puneeth said from below. "Hurry up, and just push the tiles off."

"Okay," Viren grunted. He leaned forward to push the adjoining tiles off, and they went down without too much effort. There was now a good size hole in the tiles above.

"Hold on to the table tight, guys," he called out. "I'm going to try pulling myself up through the hole."

"We got it, go on."

Viren pulled up. It was harder than it looked. The beams were too close to get a proper leverage up, and he couldn't stretch out his hands properly. He struggled up until he was partway through, with his head just above the tiles and out in the sun. But from here, he couldn't see anything inside the room. He tried to get a better grip on the beams again, but couldn't quite do it.

"Puneeth, can you…" he began, but then saw what was happening outside. His mouth dropped open.

The village was on fire. The flames were, for now, at the far side of the village, close to the jungle, but they seemed to be spreading fast. Dark clouds were beginning to billow up, carrying bits of ash along with them.

"Puneeth! Ramya! The village is on fire!" He shouted. "Can you hear me?"

There was a low murmuring sound from below, but he couldn't make out what they were saying.

"Speak up, will you!" He shouted again. It didn't feel like they'd heard him. He would anyhow not be able to get all the way out of here without them pushing him, so he had to go down to tell them to do it.

There was a tug on his leg - a gentle pull at his pant first, then gripping his leg just above the ankle and pulling firmly.

"Wait, I'm coming down!" He yelled, and began to lever himself down, out of the hole. The hold on his leg didn't slacken, in fact increased to the point where it became difficult to raise it. "Stop that, Puneeth!" He said once more, as loudly as he could.

He managed to get down about halfway through the beams, and, for a moment, was low enough to look down into the room.

It wasn't Puneeth gripping his leg. It was one of the villagers, staring grimly up at him. Light streamed into the room from the open door, and there were now at least four or five rough-looking men crowded into the place. Puneeth and Ramya were standing off a bit, looking up at him, along with the villagers.

He opened his mouth to say something, and at the same time, must have instinctively tried to pull his leg up, because the man holding him pulled down sharply, and he lost his balance completely, losing his grip on the wooden beams, hitting his head on them, and falling onto his back onto the topmost table, which, of course, broke up and took him down in an untidy heap. A searing pain went through his shoulder where the broken wood slashed into it.

"Viren!" He vaguely heard Arpita scream out, before he hit his head on the floor, too, and lost consciousness.

How long had he been out? He wasn't sure. Viren put a hand gently to the back of his head, where it hurt like hell.

Why was it so dark? He blinked, trying to adjust his eyes. He was lying down on a really uncomfortable floor. Right above him was Arpita, looking ghastly but still conscious, watching him worriedly. It was... night already? It was dark... there were lights flashing about in the room... For a moment the room vibrated, shaking the stone walls.

Stone walls? He sat up quickly, sending his head pounding. "Uh..."

Puneeth turned to him. "You're awake, thank God! Can you stand?"

"I... think so." His vision was focusing. They were in a dark room, lit only by the flickering light on Puneeth's lighter. They were walking along the walls, tapping and patting on the stones. "Where are we?"

"You got hurt really bad when you fell down, man. You were totally out." Puneeth stopped and came to him, sitting down next to Arpita. At the motion, Arpita seemed to startle awake and focus on Viren. Her eyes filled with tears. She leaned forward and held one of Viren's hands. Her hands were very hot.

"Viren…" she was sobbing now. "Viren… what has happened to us? Viren…"

Trying to ignore his head, Viren shifted over and gave Arpita a half-hug. "We'll be okay, Arpu… don't worry, we just need to break out of the roof again…"

"We aren't in our room, Viren," Puneeth said. "They took us out of it, to the basement under the temple."

Viren stared at him, his brain putting the pieces together… the stone walls, the uncomfortable floor… he ran a hand over the ground again, recognizing the metal braces that Gowri had shown them.… When was it, yesterday? Just yesterday?

The room seemed to vibrate again. His head pulsed. "Is the… room shaking?"

"Yes, it is. Not sure why. They dragged us into the room and locked it from the outside. The priest was there, too…"

"I saw… the village was on fire, when I was up on the roof."

"Yes, we saw it too, when they got us here. But I doubt they put us in here for our protection…"

Ramya called out just then. "Puneeth! Look!" She was pulling at the wooden panel on the far wall.

Puneeth went over to see. The wood was rotten in places, and Ramya had managed to pull an iron bracket from the ground and tug a couple of strips away.

There was an open space on the other side, instead of the earth or stone they'd expected.

"I think we could go through this opening if we get all the wood out," Ramya was saying. "It's soft and rotten, anyway… wonder where it leads?"

"Anything's better than here. Viren! Arpita! Hang on, we're figuring this out!" Puneeth called, levering another brace out of the ground. He set to work, getting the window - was that what it was? - open.

It took the two of them only about five minutes to get it done. Beyond the opening, it was pitch-dark, as expected, and with a strange tang to the air. Puneeth stretched out to look around with the little light he had. It was a broad passage, with rough earthen walls, perpendicular to their current room. On the two ends, it was too dark to see where they led. Below, the ground was muddy, with rivulets of water flowing along.

They went back to Viren and Arpita to get them. Viren was able to stand, though dizzy. Arpita's fever was steadily bad, and she was having trouble walking, though seeing Viren awake had calmed her down somewhat.

"Puneeth…. Where does that tunnel go?" Viren asked weakly as they approached.

"I don't know, man… but it's got to be better than being stuck in this room here," Puneeth said.

"Are there snakes there?" Arpita suddenly asked. Puneeth turned to look at her.

"They seem to be coming out everywhere, maybe this is where…" she was continuing, voice fading in and out.

It made sense. Puneeth bent himself through the opening again to look. The rivulets of water made a steady, low noise that would mask other sounds, but as far as Puneeth could see, there were no snakes, or other creatures, in the passage. He came back out and reported to the others.

"There's no other way out. That passage should have an opening somewhere. Don't see any snakes," he said.

Finally, Ramya said, "Okay… let's try. Viren, can you stand?"

Viren nodded and struggled to his feet. Puneeth grabbed an arm to help him up. With Viren on one side, lighter on the other, Puneeth maneuvered to the opening, and helped Viren through. Then, he and Ramya helped Arpita through before they went through themselves.

The water running under their feet was cold, and Arpita was shivering as she stood there. The passage was wide and high enough for all of them to stand comfortably. On either side it extended out into unknown pitch darkness.

"Which way?" Puneeth asked.

Ramya was calculating in her head. "That way," she pointed to their right. "If I remember the orientation of the room we came from, the temple is that way, away from the village."

"Okay…"

They proceeded cautiously, sticking close together as they went. The faint flame flickered on the stone walls and glittered on the rivulets of water below them.

"What... what is this place anyway?" Arpita whispered. In the silence of the passage, her voice seemed too loud.

"It might be another exit from the temple, I think... like a way to save the idol from invaders or something. They had them in the large temples long ago..." Ramya whispered back.

They'd hardly begun walking when the passage curved, widening into a broader space. The echo of their footsteps changed, too, as the ground beneath them turned to stone paving. They paused, trying to get their bearings again. Viren stumbled and sat down where he was, uncaring of the water that flowed under him, wetting him and making him shiver.

Puneeth cautiously waved the lighter around. The chamber was roughly circular, about sixty feet wide, with the walls barely visible in the faint light. All of it paved, walls and floor, with ancient, rough, stone. A musty, sealed-off smell lingered around them.

From the centre of the chamber sprouted a black pillar, going all the way up to the ceiling and going through it. At its very base the pillar split, becoming two thinner prongs as it disappeared into the ground. Around the pillar was a recessed pit, about a foot deep and six feet wide, filled with water and overflowing into the chamber. This was, Puneeth thought, the source of the rivulets flowing down the passage.

"Puneeth..." Ramya said from behind him. "That pillar... it's octagonal, right?"

He couldn't see for sure, so he stepped closer to the pillar and saw the light glint off the straight edges and surfaces. "Yes, it is."

"That means we're right below the temple now… that's the pillar we saw coming out of the ground, remember?"

Puneeth looked upwards to the pillar disappearing into the ceiling. He nodded, the movement making the lighter flame flicker.

"And that splitting into two… does it remind anyone of anything?"

"Yes," he said simply. He was looking at a mural on the wall, barely visible in the dim light. A snake catcher, a Havadiga, held a staff with a split at the far end. The split - no, it was a pin, shaped a bit like an upside down catapult, one stick splitting into two, held a writhing snake in place. More inscriptions in Hale Kannada, but the meaning was clear. They turned around to look at the pillar - the giant Chimta that had done its work for so many centuries. And now, it was breaking up.

The ground shuddered under them. Here in this chamber, the vibration was more pronounced. Arpita struggled to stay on her feet. The water in the centre pit splashed around, and some of it broke free to join the little streams flowing at their feet.

Puneeth bent down to look. The water was coming up in between the stone paving, and the stones themselves were loose and falling out of place. As he watched, the gap between them widened a little more, and water spurted.

"Guys... I think the water flow is increasing here. Let's go the other way?" He said, still staring at the pillar and the pool around it. "There's no exit from here."

"Why did they build this chamber? Did they really think it would –" Arpita was looking around her.

"Never mind! Let's get out of here..."

Arpita was sagging from weariness. Ramya pulled her upright, with an arm around her, and they began to turn around. Viren leaned on a wall, trying to stand up again.

Suddenly Arpita stood up straight, pushing Ramya off with unexpected force, sending her to the floor. "Arpita!" Ramya shouted, "What happened?"

Arpita was silent, staring off into space. Viren and Puneeth rushed towards her, Viren grabbing at her hand, which was stiff and unyielding. "Arpu! Arpu! What's going on?"

Puneeth bent down to look. "Did something bite her, or..."

Arpita began to speak. Not her own voice. It was gravelly and musty, as if unused to talking, and male.

"One boon I grant you, for doing my bidding... one boon..." The voice was loud, and echoed in the chamber.

"Arpu! Arpu!" Viren was still shouting, unnerved by the voice coming from her. But Arpita was still standing still and stiff, taking no notice of anyone.

"My boon is this: I will let you scurry out of my way when I march through my chambers. Because you have done my bidding."

Ramya registered the words first. "Chambers? What chambers?"

"Go Now. My patience is sorely tested already."

"These rooms and tunnels, I guess... but where do we go?" Puneeth replied.

"I think...we should go back into our first room..." Viren said. He was still unsteady on his feet, but he looked a little better than when he'd woken up.

"Perhaps..." Ramya said.

Right then, the strongest vibration yet shook the room. Puneeth looked back, to see the water boiling with pressure in the circular pool, and a couple of paving stones actually *jump up* in the air as the base of the pool twisted out of shape.

"We can't stay here! Quickly, let's get back into the room, before something happens!" No one knew exactly what was going to happen, but they didn't want to stay around to find out.

"Hurry, hurry..." Arpita said then, collapsing into a heap. It was her own voice again. Ramya helped her up, and the two of them hobbled back towards the passage they'd come from.

Behind them, more water splashed. The ground vibrated again, even stronger. It paused for a second, and then shook hard enough to start juddering the stone paving out of the earth.

Viren almost tripped on the uneven ground, but held on to Puneeth just in time. Ahead of them, Arpita and Ramya had reached the hole in the wall, their exit to the room, and Ramya was helping the other in.

The sound behind them changed and increased. The ground was shaking almost continuously now, the water flow under their feet getting faster. Viren idly wondered where all the water could be going, but then there was a noise like thunder, echoing in the chamber, and Puneeth lost his balance. The lighter went out. He could hear it skittering across the mud, all but out of his reach now.

Suddenly they were in total darkness. Ahead of them, Ramya cried out in alarm. "Ramya, are you okay?" Puneeth called, but there was no answer.

"Come on, Viren!" Puneeth huffed as he and Viren moved faster in the dark, feeling along the wall.

A second later, Puneeth realized he could see the wall. He looked quickly around him for the source of light. From behind them, it looked like something had been lit in the chamber, though he couldn't see what.

They reached the hole in the wall. Puneeth pushed Viren through as quiclyk as he could, and then stuck his head in, asking, "Ramya, are you there? Are you okay?"

"Yeah, we're good. Arpita fell down, but she'll be okay. Hurry, come through!"

"Yeah…"

For a moment, before he climbed through the hole, Puneeth looked behind him. Stones were falling from the walls of the passage, and even from the ceiling. The chamber was definitely brighter now, and the colour of the light was like… daylight. And there was something else.

He screamed out loud, "Get away from the hole! The ceiling's falling in the chamber!"

"Oh my God!" Viren shouted, and then they were crawling away from the opening, making space for Puneeth to dive, head-first, through the hole and out of the passage. He landed gracelessly on the ground, tearing the skin on his hands and chin from the metal bits he scraped against.

He struggled to get up, crawling quickly away from the wall, towards the far end. His heart was thudding hard in his ears. The others were already there, backed up onto the couple of steps next to the entrance door.

"You saw the ceiling falling?" Viren asked him in a whisper as he sat down next to them.

"No, just the daylight coming from above," he replied. "But I think I saw something worse…"

He stopped for a moment, wondering whether to tell them. "You remember the pit with the pillar, where the water was coming out from the stones? I'm pretty sure that whole pit was breaking up when I saw it last, the floor cracking up. And, just before I got out of the passage… something… was coming out of that pit. Something big and black…"

"Yes…. it's him," Arpita said in a voice full of awe. "Thakshaka… the lord of the snakes… he's free. Finally." She clung to Viren, shuddering.

Outside in the passage, the sound of water, and the sound of falling rock, had been growing. Now, another sound, of something big moving, was rising above the others. The ground shook so badly that stone began to fall even in the room they were in, raising dust.

The hole in the wall was clearly visible now, with light shining through from it. Motes of dust floated in the gap.

"I…" Ramya began to say, and then there was another sound out in the passage. Something pushing against the walls, something pushing the walls out of the way, as if irked by the narrowness of them, deciding that it was time. The four of them huddled together, quietened by the sound…

And then… it was there. For a microsecond a great flashing eye, golden and reptilian, crossed their window, ignoring them regally, and then it was replaced by a black wall of glittering scales, moving swiftly along the passage, faster than any man could walk. They could not see the top of the creature, only its side as it moved, but as it undulated through the passage, the light seemed to flicker.

It felt like an age had passed, and yet, the scales continued to move, impossibly large. The space they were in felt tiny in comparison to what they were seeing. With one corner of his mind, Puneeth wondered what would happen if it - him - had decided to turn into their room, destroying it and them just by his sheer size, barely even noticing them.

There was a booming sound approaching them, a rhythmic pounding as if of a wrecking ball moving along the passage. "You hear that?" Viren whispered. The whole room was shaking in time to the booms.

"Yes…" Ramya responded, her eyes still on the moving scales. The booming sound was now closer, ever closer, and now it was right next to their room, and now it was…

The wall opposite them, the one with the hole, smashed inwards with a deafening sound. The giant body of the snake, undulating, was visible beyond it, careening into the room and then withdrawing into the passage. The roof of the room collapsed on the far side once the wall was gone, and now daylight streamed in, dazzling them all. Dust floated in the air, settling on them as they sat there, stunned.

A few more seconds later, and the creature was gone. They could still hear in the distance.

"How long is that passage?" Viren finally asked.

"It probably goes all the way to the lake," Puneeth said. "All the way under the village. I think we should get out of here now."

Ahead of them, the fall of the rocks had created a pile of rubble that reached the break in the ceiling. "We can climb up that and get out," he continued.

"No… what if he's up there, waiting?" Arpita said, shrinking back. "Waiting for us?"

"We can't stay here forever, Arpu," Viren said gently. "We have to do something."

"Do something?" She said, eyes wide. "About him? He's a king, a god! He could look at us and turn us into ashes! Don't you understand?"

"I meant just get away from here, Arpu," he said, taking her hand and squeezing it. "I don't know what's going to happen here, but we have to get away." In the gray, vague daylight, his face was remarkably calm. "Take it one step at a time."

She looked from him, to the passage, and back, again, and closed her eyes, seeming to calm down. Then, head bowed, she nodded.

They stood up and made their way to the rubble. Puneeth and Ramya supported the other two up the irregular stones out into the light. They stood there, assessing their next step.

Ahead of them, the village was completely destroyed. Parts of it were still on fire; other houses had collapsed into irregular ruins of burnt brick and charred wood. The streets were strewn with abandoned items, clothes here and there, a brass pot, a bag that had burst open, strewing its contents onto the earth. And in between them, some burnt, some struck with whatever available, were snakes. Most dead, a few still moving slowly. Puneeth watched one particularly large snake, black and red, slide down from the roof of a burnt house onto the street and glide away.

There were no people around. A crashing sound came from behind them; it was the temple collapsing in fire as well.

"Look," Ramya pointed. "That's the path Thakshak went." A path along the ground was disturbed, sunk at places, with large holes and cracks that revealed the tunnel underneath.

"See, it does seem to be heading towards the lake," Puneeth said.

"Let's check the car," Viren said. "Maybe the repair guys came and fixed it. Or at least get our luggage and some food."

The car was burnt, windows smashed and the seats torn in a frenzy. They made their way to the choultry, which was miraculously unburnt in the fire. But the villagers had rampaged through the rooms, searching for valuables and money in the luggage and throwing things about. Keeping an eye out for snakes, they looked for something to eat. There was a packet of theplas that Arpita had packed for an emergency, and they ate it hungrily, standing around the room. The eerie silence around them had them all on edge.

Ramya found a small stash of money she'd hidden in a suitcase and took that out. "We get out of here now, right?"

"Yes," Puneeth said. "Who knows what's going to happen here next."

Something crashed in the next room - Gowri's room. They looked at each other. "Is she back?"

"I'll check," Viren said.

"No, wait, we'll all go together," Arpita said hurriedly. "Stay together."

They stepped out of the room and gathered outside the door of the next. It wasn't Gowri inside. Viren was reminded of that dream he'd had, the day before, about this very room.

It was the priest of the temple, looking the worse for wear, with dirty clothes and patches of mud on his arms, as if he'd been trampled under a stampede. He was rifling through the drawers and cupboards in Gowri's room, and didn't notice them watching him. Then, perhaps noticing the change in the light, he turned around, saw them, and stopped.

"What are you doing?" Puneeth asked loudly.

"What's it to you?" The priest responded. "The girl's gone, and so is the village. But how did you get out of the pooja room?"

"Just because she's gone, doesn't mean you can steal her stuff."

"I said, how did you get out of the room? You were supposed to be there when…" his eyes widened suddenly. The expression on his face changed.

"When what?" Viren asked.

But the priest didn't answer. He was staring… not at them, but at something behind them. Viren and the others turned around quickly, to see what it was.

At least a couple of dozen snakes were winding their way along the ground towards them. A strangled shriek escaped from Viren's mouth. They were surrounded, with no way to get past the serpents.

There was a shout from the priest behind them. Viren glanced quickly back to see the priest climbing up on a dressing table on the far end of the room. The table swayed precariously with his weight.

The snakes were much closer now, and Viren braced for the worst. They had nothing to defend themselves with. He took a step back... maybe they could get into the room and close it in time?

Arpita gripped his arm suddenly. She whispered, "Don't move... they won't attack us." His eyes still incredulously on the snakes, he whispered back, "what?"

She didn't say anything, just continued to hold his arm. Puneeth and Ramya had heard her, too, and stayed still.

The snakes went past them without pausing, several of them brushing past their shoes, making Viren shudder. He took a deep breath, fighting the panic at their touch, and slowly turned back. He was pretty sure he knew what the snakes were going to do.

They were clustered around the dressing table, working their way up. The priest, his eyes bulging with fear, was unable to make a sound. They watched him kick away one of the snakes as it crawled onto the top of the table, but it was never going to be enough. He saw them staring at the scene, and shouted, "Help me!"

Puneeth took a step forward, but Arpita said, "No! It's not for us to interfere!"

"What do you mean? They're going to kill him, and us next!"

Arpita's eyes were fiery. "It is not! For us to interfere. They earned his wrath, and now the King will do with them all what he wants. We dare not interfere!"

And it was too late by now. Two of the black snakes gained the tabletop, leapt across the surface, and had bitten the priest's legs. The man's face contorted in pain. Trying to shake them off, he screamed and kicked.

But now there were more, even more snakes winding up the table and biting the man, dangling off him like tentacles. The priest's face was ashen with shock. He collapsed to his knees, his hands ineffectually reaching out towards the silent watchers.

"You…" he said, before thudding to the floor. The snakes clustered ever closer to him, almost covering him.

"I'm going to be sick," Ramya said in a strangled voice. "Let's go."

They turned away from the door, all except Puneeth, who was still staring at the priest's body.

Viren hobbled back to him. "Come on, Puneeth… we need to go. Come…"

Puneeth, as if released from a spell, turned to Viren. "Yes… let's go." He cast a last glance into the room, and they began to walk away from the choultry.

The temple itself was burnt, the wooden substructure still on fire and the stone walls teetering. It took them a moment to notice that the black pillar, the pillar of Thakshaka, that had stood in front was broken and gone, too.

Discarded clothes, torn and broken bags were everywhere, thrown about in the mad rush to get away.

Somewhere just beyond the village, Viren had trouble walking when he tripped over a rock. Ahead of them, Arpita was being supported by Ramya as she walked. Puneeth paused to help him back up.

In a low voice so that the women wouldn't hear him, Puneeth said, "Where are all the people? They can't all have gotten away so quickly." His voice was strangled, as if holding back tears. He kept looking this way and that, as he draped Viren's arm around his shoulder for support.

"We saw what happened to the priest," Viren said quietly.

Puneeth's face wore a strange expression, "We caused all this, didn't we?"

Virean shook his head. "You heard them, they were going to abandon the village in a few months anyway. It was always going to happen. Don't overthink it."

They rounded the corner to where the highway could be seen, shimmering in the distance. "Let's get out of here," Viren said.

A cry of pain came from behind the temple courtyard wall. "Help me!"

"Was that Reddy?"

"We… have to try to help…" Puneeth said, suddenly shrugging Viren away. "We… caused all this."

"Puneeth, no! There will be snakes!"

A sob escaped Puneeth's lips. He shook his head doggedly and ran towards the voice. "Coming! Coming!"

Behind them Ramya and Arpita were shouting, too. "Puneeth, no! We can't!"

Puneeth disappeared around the courtyard wall.

Viren stood where he was for a moment, shuddering. Ramya overtook him as she ran to the scene, and he finally followed. The both of them stopped still when they saw what lay ahead.

There was no sign of Reddy or any other villager. The doorway that led down to the basement was smashed open, the doors in pieces. Snakes were boiling out of it, going towards the village and the jungle beyond.

Puneeth, wrapped up in snakes, already dead, his skin turning black, was being dragged down the steps. His face still held surprise. Even as they watched, his body disappeared into the darkness, no doubt where Reddy had gone as well.

"I told him… we were not to interfere. The Lord is not forgiving…" Arpita said, from behind them. "I told him! It's on him!"

Ramya turned around and slapped Arpita, hard. And again. Red welts appeared on Arpita's face, but her expression did not change.

"It's the law, Ramya. We're all just slaves to the Lord," she said placidly.

"Arpu, what are you saying!" Viren tried to take her hand, but she held them straight down, standing stiffly at attention.

"Obey him and you will not be harmed." Her eyes, glassy and distant, focused on them both for an instant. "Leave now if you want to live. He grows tired of your insolence."

"Come on, Arpu, we *all* have to get out of here!" Viren was struggling, trying to get her to come.

"GO. NOW." Arpita's voice changed. It was the deep male voice they'd heard in the chamber. "MY SUBJECT WILL STAY IN MY COURT." With a single, superhuman push, she sent Viren sprawling. Her gaze turned towards Ramya next, who backed away quickly.

"What… are you…" Viren sobbed. "No!"

Arpita turned and walked, unseeing, stepping through the snakes that parted for her, down into the darkness of the basement. In another moment she was gone.

Something shifted around the two of them, some change in the light, or in the sound. He hadn't been aware of when it had begun, but Viren was now aware that he wasn't being watched. A sense of dissolution overtook him. *The King had abandoned them…* he thought wildly.

A few of the larger snakes stopped suddenly, their heads rising, turning towards the two of them as they sat there.

Viren's skin prickled. "Ramya... they're looking at us!" He crawled backwards quickly, stumbling a couple of times. "Come on!"

Ramya shook her head. She was still staring at the entrance to the basement.

"They'll come for us too!" He cried, and, without waiting for her, struggled to his feet and ran. His vision clouded with tears as he made his way to the path, looking back again and again.

Far ahead of him, he could see a bus coming along the highway, and he increased his pace to try to reach the road.

He felt the absence now, an empty space in his mind, and he scurried, like a rat escaping from a snake, away from that gaze he never wanted to feel again.

Deccan Herald, August 13th, 2024

Mysterious deaths mount at Chitradurga dam site

The spate of suspected wildlife-caused deaths continues in the villages around the Bangarasagara Dam catchment areas. Police records show over 20 people reported missing, most found dead and mauled, from the villages. Wildlife experts are at a loss to identify the animals responsible, with the markings proving inconclusive for identification. Narsappa N., a hunter brought in by the government to follow the trails, believes it may be a pack of wild dogs or jackals, though locals insist they have heard no telltale sounds of such packs.

This reporter visited the site of the dam construction, and confirmed that the site is deserted even today, with workers fleeing the site leaving their belongings behind. The destruction of the village and its attendant temple in a fire, the week before, may be the cause of its desertion.

But no one in the area is willing to speak to outsiders. Though it was daytime, doors and windows of houses in nearby villages were closed, and shops had shutters down. We were all advised to leave the area quickly. One old woman said, "War is coming." We could get no further explanation.